ordinary
terrible
things

DIVORCE IS THE WORST

Written and illustrated by
Anastasia Higginbotham

THE FEMINIST PRESS
AT THE CITY UNIVERSITY OF NEW YORK
NEW YORK CITY

Published in 2015 by the Feminist Press
at the City University of New York
The Graduate Center
365 Fifth Avenue, Suite 5406
New York, NY 10016

feministpress.org

First printing January 2015

Illustration and design by Anastasia Higginbotham
Photography by Alexa Hoyer | Production by Drew Stevens

Library of Congress Cataloging-in-Publication Data is available for this title.

Manufactured by Thomson-Shore, Dexter, MI, USA; RMA41HS70, January, 2015

For the 5As,

Norman,

and JoAnn

It can come as a surprise.

5

When it does,

6

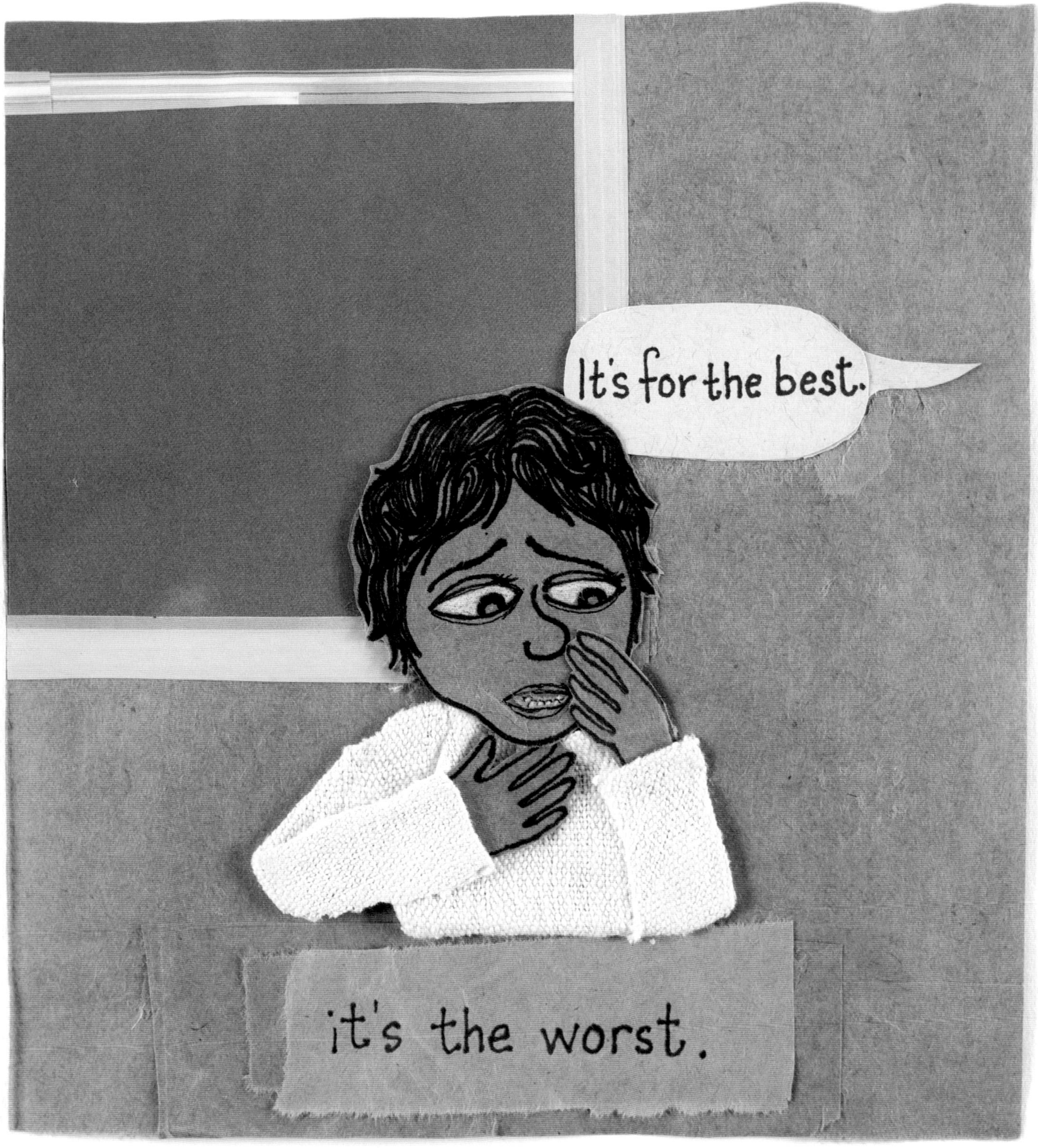
It's for the best.
it's the worst.

You may feel confused,

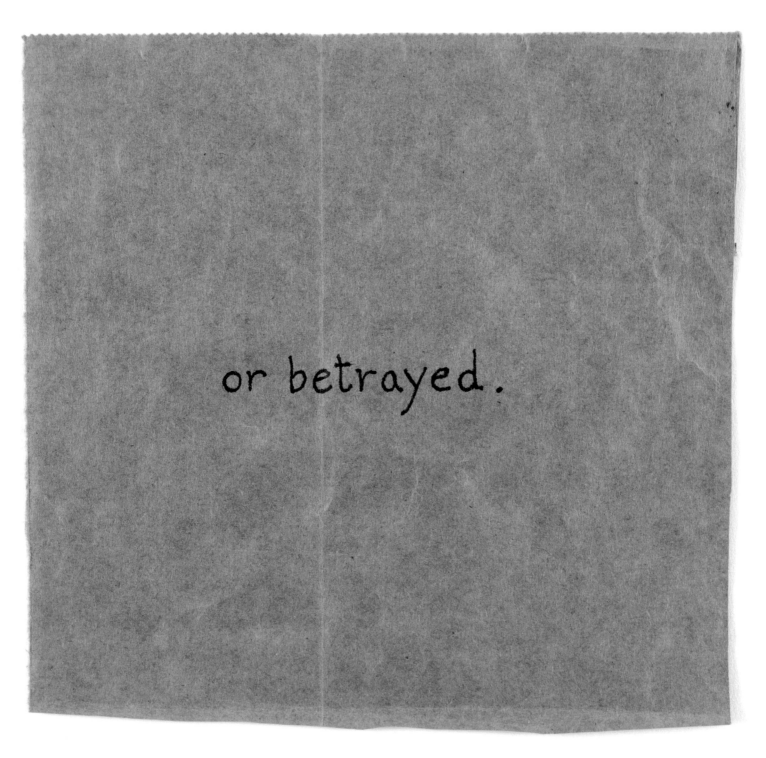

or betrayed.

You may want to run.

You may be heartbroken.

15

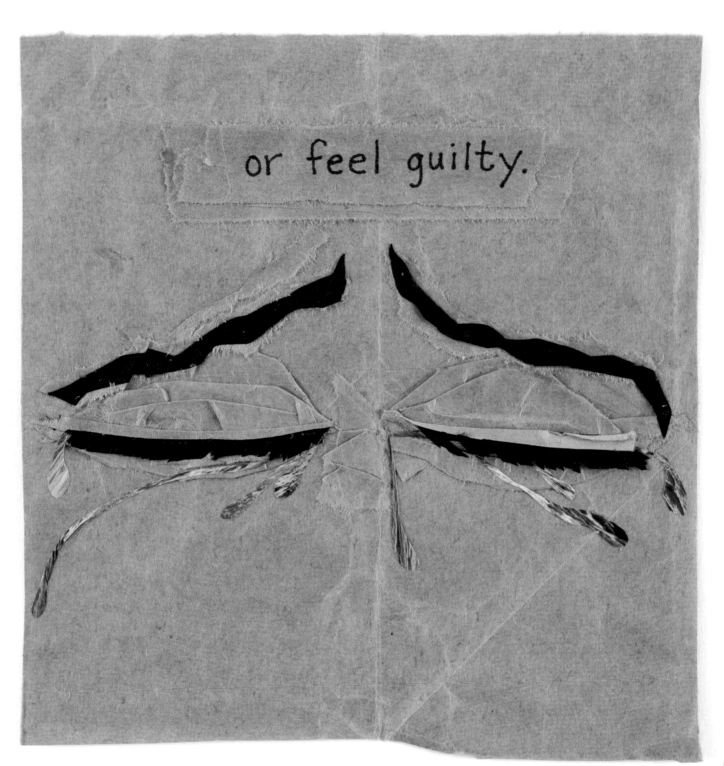

or feel guilty.

17

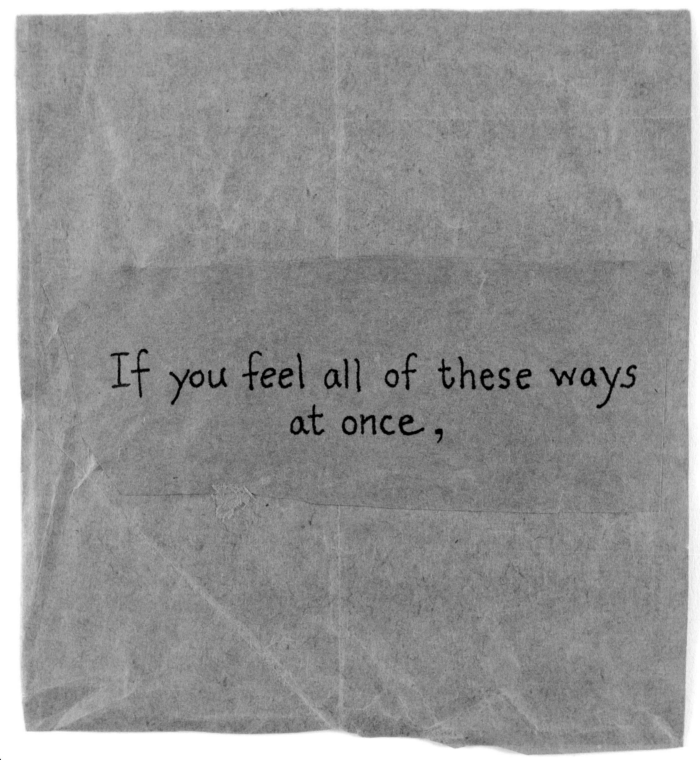

If you feel all of these ways
at once,

lie down.

We don't decide our parents' lives.

22

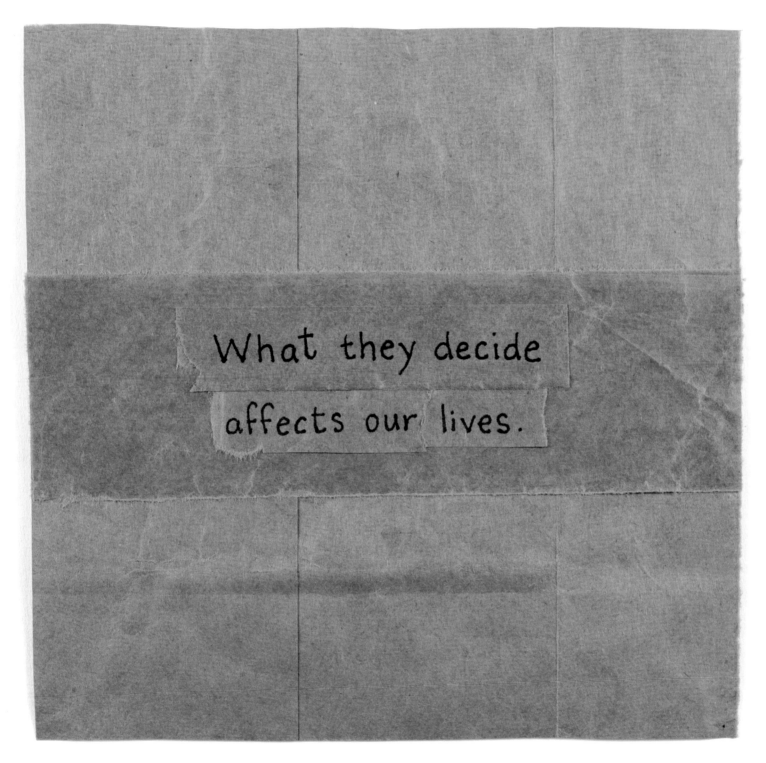

What they decide
affects our lives.

RRRINGGG!!

Divorce changes things.

You
might cry over little
things.

You might not cry...

...over big things.

33

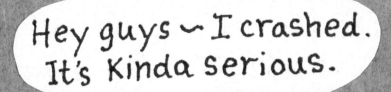

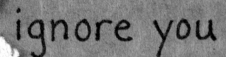

They might buy you outrageous gifts.

We love you so much!

And since your bike is wrecked...

They might introduce their friend.

Contrary to the title of this book, meeting a parent's ♥ *friend* ♥ is WORSE than the worst making it the **ABSOLUTE WORST,** even if the friend turns out to be nice, sort of, later on.

AAAAAAAH!!

They have their reasons.

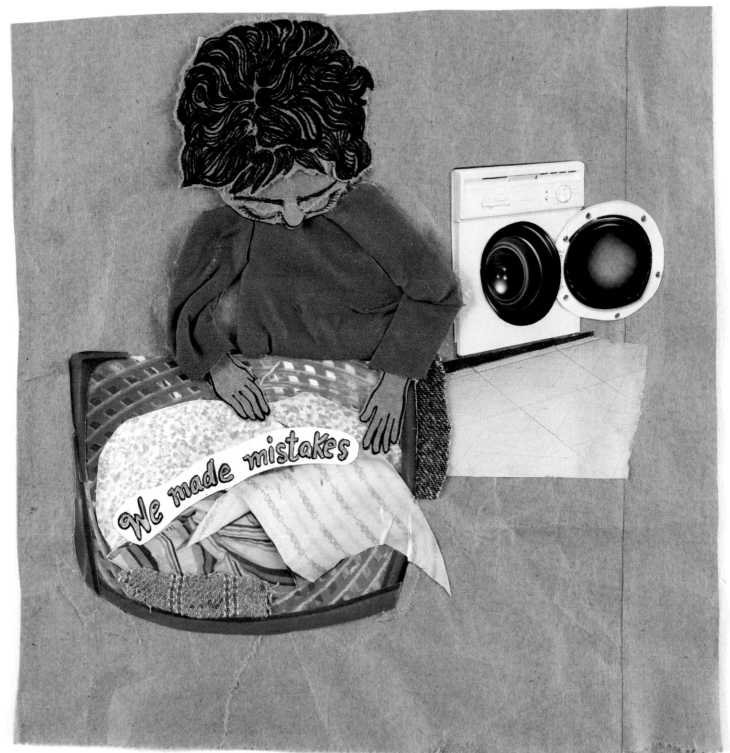

Their reasons are theirs,
not yours.

When a parent who used to be

like this

becomes more
like this,

47

Maybe a divorce is for the best
— for them.

You got your stuff
for the weekend?

Divorce can feel like being pulled in two directions at once.

Sometimes, exactly like that.

Divorce
means
your
parents

are splitting
from each other.

53

54

the end

Here is what to do with all those feelings and more:

Lay that burden down.

feel rejected by parent who moved out

wish I could sleep in my own real bed

must love my parents more — so they won't be sad

no one pays attention to me

must fix my parents' lives

there's someone new at breakfast

they're always working

I'm worried about $$$

Make a special place for them out of your way. Know your troubles as well as you can. Then let them be.

On days when your worries want to show, wear them like flags, with pride!

And when you want help to let your fear, worry, or ♥-break float away, tell someone you trust.

Help. —

You may not control everything that happens in your life,

but it's still your life, your story.

Tell it, Kid! And live it: brave and true.

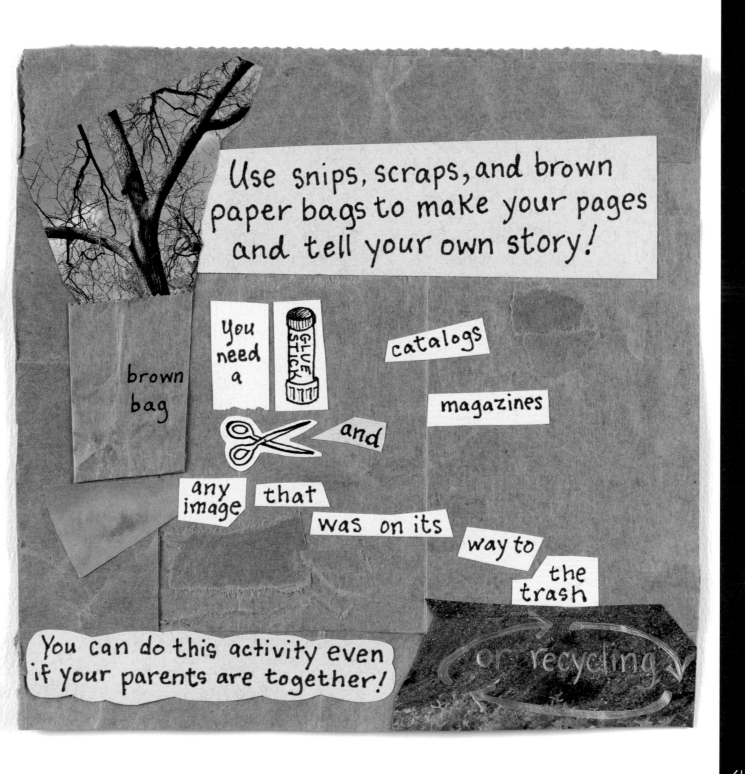

Use snips, scraps, and brown paper bags to make your pages and tell your own story!

brown bag

You need a

GLUE STICK

and

catalogs

magazines

any image that was on its way to the trash

or recycling

You can do this activity even if your parents are together!

Start by creating a place where you can be all in one piece.

Choose a sky that mirrors what you feel.

Find trees to lift you up or hide you. Trees bear witness and stand by you.

Choose the ground, rocks, roots, and grass that best support you.

And now you make YOU:

Dressed in scraps of clothes you've outgrown.

Hands

Head

Ribbon hair can be any way you like.

Anastasia Higginbotham's books about ordinary, terrible things tell stories of children who navigate trouble with their senses sharp and souls intact.

Help may come from family, counselors, teachers, and dreams — but it's the children who find their own way through.

Anastasia has been making books by hand her whole life as a way to cope with change and grow.

You CAN TOO!

ordinary
terrible
things

ordinary
terrible
things